ELIJAH THE SLAVE

Pictures by Antonio Frasconi

Farrar, Straus and Giroux
New York

A Hebrew Legend Retold by
ISAAC BASHEVIS SINGER
Translated from the Yiddish by the author and Elizabeth Shub

In ancient times, in a distant land, there was a large city where many rich men lived. It had magnificent palaces, broad avenues, parks, and gardens.

In their midst was a tiny street of broken-down houses. They had narrow windows and doorways, and their roofs leaked. In the humblest of these, there lived a holy man. Tobias was his name, and his wife was called Peninah. They had five children, three sons and two daughters.

Tobias was a scribe who copied the sacred scrolls. In this way he was able to earn a meager living.

But suddenly he was taken ill and lost the use of his right hand. Soon there was no bread in the house. The larder was so empty that even the mice ran away. There was nothing for the cat to catch. The boys could not go to school because they had no shoes. Tobias's clothes were in rags and tatters.

When the neighbors saw the family's need, they tried to help. But Tobias refused their offers, saying, "There is a God and He will help us."

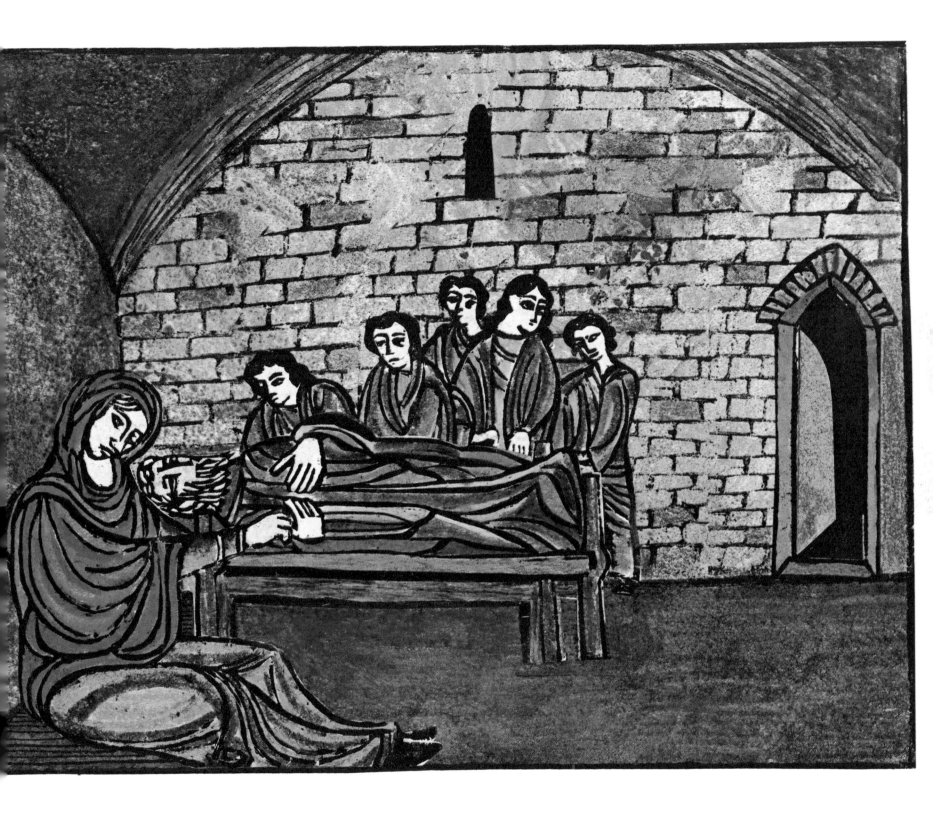

One day Tobias's wife said to him: "If God intends to help us, it better be soon. But whatever He might do, for you to just sit at home doesn't improve matters. You must go out into the city. Even while waiting for a miracle, it's good to do something. Man must begin and God will help him."

"How can I show my face among people when I have no clothes to wear?"

"Wait, my husband, and I will take care of that."

Peninah went to a neighbor and borrowed a coat, a hat, and shoes. She helped Tobias dress and truly he looked like a new man. "Now, go," Peninah said, "and luck be with you." When he left, she told the children to pray that their father would not come home with empty hands.

As Tobias approached the center of the city, a stranger stopped him. He was tall and had a white beard. He wore a long coat and carried a staff. "Peace be with you, Tobias," he said, and held out his hand. Tobias, forgetting he could not move his right hand, clasped the stranger's with it. He was baffled by this miraculous recovery.

"Who do I have the honor of greeting?" Tobias asked.

"My name is Elijah and I am your slave."

"My slave?" Tobias said in astonishment.

"Yes, your slave, sent from heaven. Take me to the marketplace and sell me to the highest bidder."

"If you come from heaven, I am *your* slave," Tobias answered. "How can a slave sell his master?"

"Do as I say," Elijah replied.

Since Elijah was a messenger from God, Tobias had no choice but to obey.

In the marketplace, many rich merchants gathered around Tobias and Elijah. Never before had a slave who looked so noble and wise been offered for sale.

The richest and most forward of the merchants addressed him. "What can you do, slave?"

"Anything you wish," Elijah said.

"Can you build a palace?"

"The most magnificent you have ever seen."

"Even more splendid than the King's?"

"More splendid—and bigger."

"Why should we believe you?" asked one of the merchants.

Elijah took a sack of wooden blocks from his pocket and with them built a miniature palace. He did it with such speed and the palace's beauty was so unusual that the merchants were dazzled.

"Can you build a real palace like this one?" the richest merchant asked.

"A better one," said Elijah.

The merchants, sensing that this slave had supernatural powers, began the bidding at once. "Ten thousand gulden," one shouted.

"Fifty thousand," called another.

"One hundred thousand," offered a third.

The highest price—800,000 gulden—was finally offered by the richest merchant, and he paid the money to Tobias.

Turning to Elijah, the merchant said, "If the real palace is as beautiful as you promise, I will make you a free man."

"Very well," Elijah replied. And to Tobias he said, "Go home and rejoice with your wife and children. Your days of poverty are over."

After giving praise to God and thanking Elijah for his goodness, Tobias returned home.

The joy of his wife and children was great.

As always, Tobias gave a tenth part of his money to the poor; and even though he was now a rich man, he decided to go back to his beloved work as a scribe.

Night came and Elijah spoke to God. "I sold myself as a slave to save your servant Tobias. I pray you now to help me build the palace."

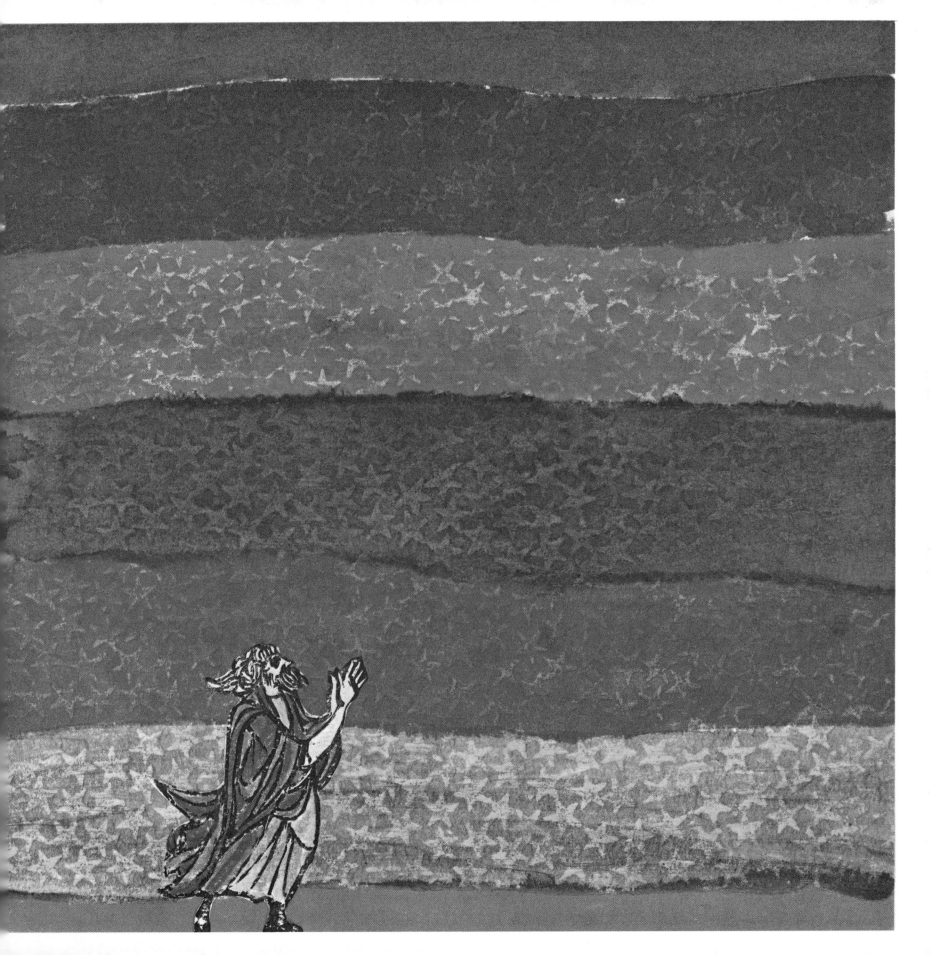

Immediately a band of angels descended from heaven. They worked all night long. When the sun rose, the palace was finished.

The rich merchant came and gazed in awe. Never had an edifice of such splendor been seen by human eyes.

"Here is your palace," Elijah said. "Keep your word and give me my freedom."

"You are free, my lord," replied the merchant and he bowed low before God's messenger.

The angels laughed.

God looked down from his seventh heaven and smiled.

The angels spread their wings and, together with Elijah, flew upward into the sky.

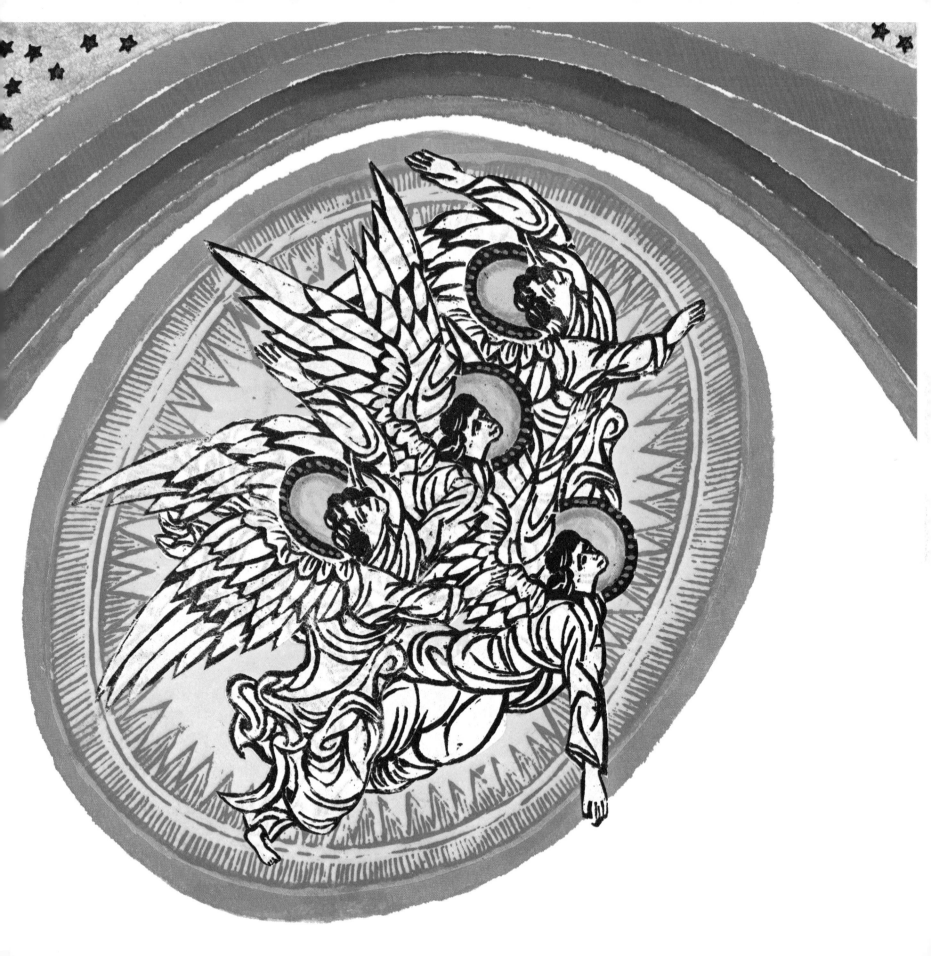